THE
TROUBLE WITH
TINK

Bath · New York · Singapore · Hong Kong · Cologne · Delhi · Melbourne

Ping! Ping! Ping! One sunny afternoon in Pixie Hollow, Tinker Bell sat in her workshop mending a dented copper pot. She had almost finished when her friend Terence appeared.

"Oh, hi, Terence. Come in," said Tink.

Terence was a dust-talent sparrow man. He handed out the fairy dust that allowed the fairies to fly and do their magic.

"Hi, Tink. I just wanted to let you know that they're starting a game of tag in the meadow," said Terence.

Tink glanced down at the pot. The dent was nearly smooth. Tink thought she could easily play tag and have time to finish her work later.

Standing up, she slipped her tinker's hammer into a loop on her belt and smiled at Terence.

"Let's go," she said.

When they arrived, the game of tag was in full swing. Games of fairy tag are very exciting. The fairies and sparrow men use their talents to try to win. When a fairy is tagged their whole talent group becomes 'it'.

As Tink and Terence joined the game they realised that dust-talent fairies were 'it'.

Tink caught sight of Terence and bolted. In a flash, Terence was after her.

Tink dove into a bush. Suddenly, the twigs in front of her closed and Tink skidded to a halt. Terence had used a flick of fairy dust to trap her.

Just then, a shout rang out: *"Hawk!"*

At once, Tink and Terence dropped down under cover as the hawk's shadow moved across. When it was gone, the fairies slowly came out of their hiding places. But the mood had changed. The game of tag was over.

"I must finish mending that pot," Tink told Terence.

Tink's fingers itched to begin working again. As she flew back to her workshop, she reached for her tinker's hammer hanging on her belt. Her fingertips touched the leather loop. Tink stopped flying. Her hammer was gone!

Tink skimmed over the ground, back the way she'd come. Her eyes darted this way and that.

When she reached the meadow, her heart sank. It just looked like a vast jungle of waving sunflowers.

Just then, her eyes fell on the bush. *Of course!* Tink thought. *I must have dropped it when I was dodging Terence.*

Tink checked everywhere, but the hammer was nowhere to be found. In fact, the hammer was already long gone. A Never magpie had spotted the shiny metal and carried it off to its nest.

The sun sank below the horizon and it became too dark to search any more.

As Tink flew home, tears of frustration rolled down her cheeks. *What will I do without my hammer?* Tink wondered.

It might seem that it should have been easy for Tink to get another tinker's hammer, but in fact, it was not. In the fairy kingdom, there is just the right amount of everything; no more, no less.

But that wasn't the only reason she was crying. Tink had a secret. She *did* have a spare hammer. But it was at Peter Pan's hideout – she had accidentally left it there quite a while before. And she was terribly scared about going back to get it.

Tink thought about Peter Pan: his wild red hair, his freckled nose and his laugh. Tink's heart ached. Remembering Peter Pan was something she almost never let herself do. Since he had brought the Wendy to Never Land, Tink and Peter had hardly spoken.

No, Tink decided. She couldn't go to Peter's for the spare hammer. It would make her too sad.

"I'll make do without it," she told herself.

Early the next morning, Tink crept out of the Home Tree and flew down to the beach. Tink picked up a reddish pebble the size and shape of a sunflower seed.

"This might work," Tink said aloud into the empty cave.

Back in her workshop, Tink used iron wire and a pinch of fairy dust to bind the flat side of the pebble to a twig. She held up her makeshift hammer and looked at it.

"It's not so bad," she said.

Taking a deep breath, Tink began to tap the copper pot.

Clank! Clank! Clank! Tink winced at the horrible sound. Each strike with the pebble hammer left a tiny dent.

Tink fought back tears. *It's no good*, she thought. *This pebble doesn't work at all!*

Suddenly, the door of Tink's workshop burst open and a fairy flew in. It was Violet, the pot's owner.

"Tink! Thank goodness you're almost done with the... Oh!" Violet exclaimed. She stopped and stared at her battered pot.

"Oh, Violet, hi. Yes, I'm, er... I'm done with the pot. That is, mostly," Tink said. She tugged nervously at her fringe.

"It looks... uh... " Violet's voice trailed off.

"It needs a couple of touch-ups, but it's perfectly good to use. Tink reassured her. "We can try it now if you like."

The door of Tink's workshop opened again. Terence came in, carrying a ladle with a twisted handle.

"Hi, Tink! I brought you a ladle to fix!" he called out. "Oh, hello, Violet! Dropping off?" he asked as he spied the pot.

"No... er, picking up," Violet said worriedly.

"Oh!" said Terence, in surprise.

Violet and Terence watched as Tink poured a bucket of water into the copper pot.

"See?" Tink said to Violet. "It's good as – "

Just then – *plink, plink, plink, plink!* One by one, tiny streams of water burst through the damaged copper.

"Oh!" Violet and Terence gasped.

Tink blushed. She had never failed to fix something before.

After a long silence, Violet said, "I can probably borrow a pot from someone else." And she hurried off.

Terence was also confused, but he was in no hurry to leave.

"Tink, you look tired," he said gently.

"I'm not tired," snapped Tink.

Suddenly, Tink was irritated with Terence. If he hadn't told her about the tag game, she never would have lost her hammer.

Terence's shoulders sagged. "Just let me know if you need anything," he said, and headed for the door.

As soon as Terence was gone, Tink flew to a nearby birch tree where a carpenter-talent sparrow man worked. He agreed to let her borrow his hammer for a while.

She began to work on a stack of pie pans. Dulcie, the baking-talent fairy who'd brought them to her, complained that her pies kept burning. Tink thought maybe the tin was too thin.

Tink worked slowly with the carpenter's big, clumsy hammer, adding an extra layer of tin to the bottom of each pan. When she was done, she looked over her work.

It's not the best job I've ever done, she thought. *But it's not so bad, either.*

Tink gathered up the pie pans and carried them to Dulcie. Dulcie was delighted to have them back.

"Don't miss tea this afternoon, Tink," she said with a wink. "I'll save you an extra-big slice of strawberry pie!"

On the way back to her workshop, Tink ran into Fawn, an animal-talent fairy with a bouncy nature.

"Tink!" Fawn cried, "Did you hear about the queen's bath? It's sprung a leak!"

Tink's eyes widened. The beautiful pewter bath was one of Queen Clarion's most prized possessions.

"Of course, the queen will want you to fix it. You're the best." Fawn grinned at Tink.

Tink grinned back, showing her deep dimples.

"I hope so, Fawn. It would be a real honour," she replied.

Tink thought about the queen's bath all afternoon as she fixed the spout on a kettle that wouldn't whistle. What kind of leak could it be? A hairline crack? Or a pinprick hole? Tink smiled, imagining the possibilities.

By the time Tink had finished fixing the kettle, it was nearly teatime, so she headed for the kitchen.

But when she arrived, a horrible smell greeted her. Tink quickly handed the kettle to one of the cooking-talent fairies and held her nose. "What is that smell?" she asked.

But the fairy just gave her a strange look and hurried off to fill the kettle with water.

Tink found Dulcie standing over several steaming pies.

"Dulcie, what's going on?" Tink asked.

"Oh, Tink," Dulcie wailed. "It's the pies. They're all coming out mincemeat."

This was indeed a kitchen disaster. Fairies hate mincemeat.

"Is there something wrong with the oven?" Tink asked.

Dulcie swallowed hard. "No, Tink," she said. "Only the pies baked in the pans that you fixed get spoiled."

Tink's mind reeled. But before she could say anything, a shrill whistle split the air. The tea water had boiled. A cooking-talent fairy poured the water into the teacups until there wasn't a drop left.

But the kettle continued to shriek.

Several fairies who were in the tearoom poked their heads around the kitchen door.

"What's all that noise?" a garden-talent fairy asked.

"It's the kettle," the cooking-talent fairy replied. "Tink fixed it, and now it won't shut up! And the pans Tink fixed are broken, too."

Everyone looked at Tink. Tink blushed deeply, Then, without thinking, she turned and fled.

15

Tink was sitting in the shade of a wild honeysuckle, deep in thought when Vidia, a fast-flying-talent fairy, landed right in front of her.

"Tinker Bell, darling," Vidia greeted her.

"Hello, Vidia," Tink replied. Of all the fairies in the kingdom, Vidia was the one Tink liked the least. Vidia was pretty, but she was selfish and mean and at the moment she was smiling in a way Tink didn't like at all.

"I'm *so* sorry to hear about your *talent*," she said.

Tink blinked. "What do you mean?"

"The rumour is that you've lost your talent."

"I haven't lost my talent," Tink growled.

"If you say so. But, sweetheart, you have to admit, your work hasn't exactly been... *inspired* lately," Vidia said with a little laugh. "But I wouldn't worry too much. I'm sure they won't make you leave the fairy kingdom *forever*."

Tink looked at her coldly. "I'm sure that would never happen, Vidia."

Vidia gave Tink a pitying smile. "Well, I guess we'll soon find out. The queen would like to see you. Goodbye, Tink."

Tink's heart raced. What could this mean? Was it really possible that she could be banished from the kingdom?

But I haven't lost my talent! Tink thought, *I've just lost my hammer.*

Tink took a deep breath and flew off to meet the queen.

Queen Clarion stood at an open window, looking at the glittering blue water of the Mermaid Lagoon in the distance.

"Tinker Bell," said the queen. "How are you feeling?"

"I'm fine," Tink replied.

"No cough? Your glow hasn't changed?" asked the queen.

"No," Tink reassured her.

"Tink, you know there are rumours..." the queen hesitated.

"They say I've lost my talent," Tink said quickly. "It's nasty gossip – and untrue. It's just that – " Tink stopped.

She was afraid that if she told Queen Clarion about her missing hammer, the queen would think she was irresponsible.

The queen looked into her blue eyes. "Tink," she said, "is there anything you want to tell me?"

She asked so gently that Tink felt the urge to tell her everything, but instead she shook her head.

"No," she said. "I'm sorry my pots and pans haven't been very good lately. I'll try to do better."

Queen Clarion knew something was wrong, but she could see that Tink didn't want to tell her. "Very well," she said.

Outside, Tink felt better. The meeting with the queen had been nothing to worry about after all. *All I have to do now is find a new hammer,* Tink thought.

Later in the tearoom, Tink joined the other pots-and-pans fairies at their table.

"It's a crack, I'll bet," a fairy named Zuzu was saying.

"But it could be a problem with the drain," said Angus.

Tink leaned forward. "What's everyone talking about?"

"About the queen's bath," Zuzu explained. "She's asked us to fix it tomorrow"

"Oh!" said Tink. Suddenly, she realised that the queen had not asked *her* to fix the bath.

Tink slipped away from the table unnoticed. Outside, she flew to the uppermost branches of the Home Tree. She didn't want to go back to her workshop – there were pots and pans waiting to be fixed.

"Maybe it's true that I've lost my talent," Tink said to the stars. "If I don't have a hammer, then I can't fix things. And if I can't fix things, it's just like having no talent at all."

"Tink," said a voice.

Terence was standing behind her on the branch.

"I saw you leave the tearoom. Are you all right? Everyone is saying that... " He paused.

"That I've lost my talent," Tink finished for him.

22

Tink sighed. "Maybe they're right, Terence. I can't seem to fix anything any more."

"I don't believe that," he told her. "You're the best pots-and-pans fairy in the kingdom. Tink," Terence asked gently, "what's really going on?"

Tink hesitated. "I lost my hammer," she blurted at last.

Tink felt so relieved, it was as if she'd let out a huge breath.

"Is that all it is?" Terence said. He almost laughed. "But you could borrow a hammer," he suggested.

Tink told Terence about the hammer she'd made from a pebble and the one she'd borrowed from the carpenter fairy.

"It's no good," she said. "I need a tinker's hammer."

"Maybe there's a spare – " Terence began.

"I *have* a spare," Tink wailed. "But it's... I... I left it at Peter Pan's hideout."

They sat silently for a moment, looking up at the stars.

"I could go with you," Terence said at last. "To Peter Pan's, I mean."

"You would do that?" she asked.

"I'm your friend," said Terence. "You don't even need to ask." And he gave Tink a sparkling smile.

23

The next morning, Tink and Terence left Pixie Hollow as the sun was rising. Tink looked down at the island below her. Every rock, meadow and hill reminded her of some adventure. Of course, they also reminded her of Peter.

Tink felt a flutter of nervousness. How would it be to see him? What if the Wendy was there, or Peter ignored her again?

When Tink reached the densest, darkest part of the forest, she began to glide down in a spiral. Terence followed her.

They plunged through a canopy of fig trees and landed on a mushroom. After they had rested for a moment, Tink sprang up and flew to a hollow in the trunk of a nearby jackfruit tree.

"This is the entrance to the hideout!" said Tink.

Terence followed Tink as she flew down the hollow trunk. They came out in an underground den.

Terence looked around. Cobwebs and string hammocks dangled from the ceiling and slingshots, socks and dirty coconut-shell bowls were scattered on the ground. But there was no one in sight.

He's not home, Tink thought. She felt both disappointed and relieved.

Just then, they heard whistling coming from the back of the den.

Tink and Terence flew towards the sound. When they rounded the corner, Terence saw a freckled boy with a mop of red hair. He was whistling as he sat carving a fishing hook.

Tink saw her old friend, Peter Pan.

Taking a deep breath, Tink said, "Hello, Peter."

Peter lifted his head and a bright smile lit his face.

"Tink!" he cried. "It's awful great to see you!"

"Hello, Peter," Tink replied. "Meet my friend Terence."

"A boy pixie! Fantastic!" Peter cried, turning to Terence.

The grin on his face was so wide it was impossible not to like Peter Pan.

Tink decided to get straight to the point. "You – er – I don't suppose you've still got my hammer." Tink stammered.

Peter reached over and lifted the lid of an old cigar box. He took out a small object and held it out towards Tink.

"Oh!" Tink gasped. "You've got it!"

"I saved it for you, Tink," Peter said proudly.

Tink smiled. She had discovered that it wasn't so hard to see Peter, after all!

Tink took the hammer. It fitted perfectly in her hand. Then, Tink turned to Peter and said, "It's been so good to see you, Peter. But we have to go back to the fairy kingdom now."

Peter looked at her in surprise. "What? Already? What about a game of hide-and-seek?"

Tink shook her head. She was glad to realise that she didn't want to stay, not for hide-and-seek or anything else. She wanted to get back to Pixie Hollow, where she belonged.

Tink kissed the bridge of Peter's freckled nose. "I'll come back soon to visit," she promised. And she meant it.

Then, taking Terence's hand, she flew back out of the jackfruit tree and into the forest. They headed back to the fairy kingdom together.

"That was easy," grinned Terence.

Tink grinned back. What a good friend Terence was.

"Now, how will we convince everyone that you have got your talent back?" he asked.

Tink thought for a moment. "I have an idea," she said.

When they got to the Home Tree, Tink went straight to Queen Clarion's quarters.

One of the queen's attendants opened the door.

"I've come to fix the queen's bath," Tink told her.

Terence, who was standing behind Tink, grinned. Tink was clever. This was the perfect way to prove that her talent was back. Terence didn't doubt that Tink could fix the bath.

But the attendant hesitated. Everyone had heard about Tink and her talent. Just then, the queen stepped forward.

"Come in, Tink," she said.

"I've come to fix your bath," Tink repeated.

The queen looked at Tink and she saw a fierce certainty in her eyes that hadn't been there the day before.

The queen nodded. "Take Tink to the bath," she told her attendant.

The surprised attendant turned and began to lead Tink away. Just before Tink left, Terence grabbed her hand.

"Good luck," he said.

Tink touched her hammer and gave his hand a squeeze.

"I don't need it!" she said.

THE END